THE LEGEND OF MORVIDUS CONTINUES

THE BEARS' FAMILY

Written by Rachael Wong

Illustrated by Jim Troughton

BREWIN BOOKS

First published by
Brewin Books Ltd, 19 Enfield Ind. Estate,
Redditch, Worcestershire B97 6BY in 2020

www.brewinbooks.com

ISBN: 978-1-85858-715-8

A Cataloguing in Publication Record
for this title is available from the British Library.

Typeset in Jerky Tash.
Printed in the UK by
W&G Baird Ltd.

All over the world,

Wherever they play,

Stars of tomorrow

Are starting today.

All royalties from this book will be given to

Queen Elizabeth Hospital Birmingham Charity and NSPCC Childline,

via the Edgbaston Foundation.

FOREWORD

Chris Woakes

Warwickshire and
England All Rounder

Firstly, I would like to thank Jim for the opportunity to write the Foreword for this book about the Warwickshire Bear.

It is a huge honour to represent the Warwickshire Bear every day. The Bear means so much more than just a cricket team. I have been lucky enough to represent the Warwickshire Bear for around 20 years and it will always have a place in my heart.

We have a saying at the club – 'Once a Bear, always a Bear'. Being part of the Bears' family is something no one takes for granted and we are all extremely lucky to be part of it.

As players and staff, we are a small part of the Bears' incredible long history and all we hope is that we can work to leave it in a better place than when we were first given that golden opportunity to become a Bear.

My family are Warwickshire fans and they made huge sacrifices in helping me to become a Warwickshire Bear. It fills me with so much pride that I am part of the Warwickshire family too, and I play knowing they are also proud every time I get the opportunity to play.

Jim, skipper, coach… thanks again. I hope you all enjoy your association with the Bear as much as I have and will continue to do so.

All the best,

Chris Woakes

FOREWORD

Issy Wong

Birmingham Bears Bowler

Having been a Bear since I was nine years old, I was really happy to be asked to write a Foreword for this new story about the origin of the Bear on the Warwickshire badge – particularly as I made a cameo appearance in the first Morvidus book when I was twelve.

I like the part of this story where Morvidus and his sister Morwenna play turnip ball. Turnip ball bears a striking resemblance to cricket and I like to think I play cricket just like Morwenna plays turnip ball.

This is also a story about looking after each other: something we do in the Warwickshire family, and of course it is what the NHS is doing for us all at the current time. Thank you to the NHS staff who are looking after us, from everyone at Warwickshire CCC.

Issy Wong

This story came to life during the COVID-19 pandemic in Spring 2020. It is dedicated to our amazing NHS staff. Thank you for your strength and courage on behalf of everyone at Warwickshire CCC and the Warwickshire cricket family.

Alex's three favourite things in life were his family, playing cricket, and his bedtime story. Most nights, Alex would ask for the story of Morvidus. Morvidus was a brave warrior who had pulled a tree out of the ground in the forest to fight a giant, and then added the picture of the tree to his shield.

"You know when Morvidus put the tree on his shield?" Alex asked Dad one night.

"Yes," replied Dad. "We call it a ragged staff nowadays. It's on the Warwickshire badge."

"I know that," continued Alex. "But the picture of the Bear was already on his shield. How did that get there? Is there a story about that too?"

Dad looked at Alex's eager face. Poor Alex hadn't been able to go out and play cricket with his friends for a long time and Dad wanted to cheer him up. "Well, the answer to that is 'yes'. There is a story. Would you like to hear it now?"

Alex almost leapt out of bed in delight.

"Steady on," laughed Dad, as he settled back down on the bedroom floor to start the next story.

When Morvidus was a boy in ancient Warwickshire, his favourite things in life were his family, playing turnip ball with his sister Morwenna, and hearing stories about brave warriors. Morvidus and Morwenna had invented the game of turnip ball themselves. The rules were very simple: one person threw a turnip as hard as they could at the other person. This other person had to hit the turnip as far as they could with a big stick, ideally into the bushes at the end of the field.

Morvidus and Morwenna could both throw and hit a turnip very hard. Each of them had a favourite stick they used (kept hidden from the other one the rest of the time). Their father, Sir Hugh, had given them one turnip from the barn to play with, but he said the rest of the turnips were needed to feed the family during the winter. So, every time Morvidus or Morwenna hit the turnip into the bushes, they had to go and find it.

One day, Morvidus and Morwenna were in the forest collecting berries for their mother, Lady Carmen. Well, they were meant to be collecting berries but of course they were actually playing a fierce game of turnip ball.

Morvidus threw the turnip really hard at Morwenna. It hit the middle of her stick and she whacked it hard, right into the heart of the forest, beyond the danger sign warning people about monsters and strange beasts.

Morvidus groaned. The children knew they shouldn't go beyond the warning sign but they needed to find their one and only turnip. With only a moment's hesitation, Morvidus and Morwenna set off to find their turnip.

The children were so busy looking for the turnip, they didn't hear the snap of twigs or the rustling bushes. What they did hear, though, was what came next – the deafening roar of an enormous angry bear as it drew itself up, right in front of them, ready to attack.

"Run!" yelled Morvidus. "Over here. Quickly. Up this tree."

Brother and sister raced away from the angry bear and climbed a large oak tree like a couple of squirrels. The bear paced around the bottom of the tree, growling up at the children. Luckily this was not the type of bear that climbed trees.

Morvidus and Morwenna looked around helplessly. What could they do? The bear had them trapped. The children knew they would have to stay in the tree until the bear went away, or their parents came to look for them. Then the bear would attack their parents and this worried the children as neither Sir Hugh nor Lady Carmen were very good at climbing trees.

Suddenly, Morwenna spotted something. "Look," she whispered to Morvidus. "Over there, behind those bushes. Can you see it? It looks like a baby bear, stuck in a hunting trap."

Morvidus looked closely. Morwenna was right; he could see a pit, which a small bear had fallen into. It was helpless at the bottom with a rope around its neck. Morvidus felt sorry for the young bear. He also realised the big bear must be its parent and wasn't going to go away without its cub.

"Well," whispered Morvidus to Morwenna, "There's only one thing we can do. Somehow, we'll have to go and free that bear cub from the trap."

"What?" hissed Morwenna, angrily. "Are you mad?"

"Listen," Morvidus replied softly. "You keep the bear distracted. I am going to climb further up the tree, into the leaves, where the bear can't see me. Then I am going to climb from tree to tree and come down over there behind the trap."

Before Morwenna could argue with him, Morvidus disappeared up the tree, leaving Morwenna to occupy the big bear. "Well," she said to herself, "Morvidus isn't going to have all the excitement here." So Morwenna hung by her knees from the branch and swung down just above the bear's head.

The bear lashed up at Morwenna with his fearsome claws, snarling with rage. Twice more Morwenna swung down. Her legs were tired but she had to keep going because she could see Morvidus had just climbed down from the tree behind the trapped cub. The angry grown up bear must not see Morvidus.

Morvidus knew he had to work quickly if he was to set the cub free before the big bear saw him. Hopping down into the trap, Morvidus pulled out his hunting knife and started cutting the rope around the cub's neck. It was slow work and the bear cub was struggling all the time, as it didn't understand that Morvidus was trying to cut it free.

Eventually, the rope was cut. Morvidus and the bear cub were, however, still stuck in the trap. Gently but firmly, Morvidus lifted the wriggling bear cub over his head, up out of the trap. The cub yelped...

Morwenna heard the bear cub yelp and saw it reappear out of the trap. Immediately the grown up bear turned round, saw the cub, and bounded over to it. Morvidus was still in the trap! Morwenna was horrified as she watched the big bear stick its head into the hole and give the most terrifying roar.

Morvidus froze with fear as the head of the grown up bear appeared above him at the entrance to the trap. Saliva dripped in rivers down from its sharp teeth. The bear's mouth was like a cave, and its breath stank. Morvidus was sure just one swipe from those giant claws would be the end of him.

The bear roared again; a slightly different roar, perhaps a softer roar? Morvidus couldn't be sure, but he had a feeling the bear was smelling him. The bear then unexpectedly took its head out of the hole.

Sitting in the tree, Morwenna watched the big bear lick the cub all over, as if checking it. When the grown up bear was satisfied all was well, the two bears slowly walked back into the depths of the forest and there was silence.

When she was sure the bears had gone, Morwenna jumped down from her tree and raced over to the trap. She was very worried about Morvidus, but when she poked her head into the trap a very complete-looking Morvidus shouted up to her, "Throw me one of those ropes, will you, so I can climb out? That was even more exciting than turnip ball, but I wouldn't want to do it every day!"

A few years later, Morvidus became a young squire. All the games of turnip ball with Morwenna had made him strong and Morvidus had become the best swordsman in the area. Morvidus also carried a massive wooden shield, heavier than most men could carry.

One day, Lord Hugh sent Morvidus to the King with an urgent message about some thieves who were attacking local villages. "Take this message to the King," he instructed Morvidus, "And beware of the thieves in the woods."

Morvidus was delighted he had been asked to deliver the message. He would now be able to meet up with Morwenna, who was serving as a shield warrior for the Queen at the King's fortress in Bagestdon.

Morvidus rode swiftly through the woods to Bagestdon. Suddenly, he spotted movement ahead of him in the trees. Morvidus managed to slow down just in time to see a rope stretched across the path; a rope that was designed to pull him off his horse. Although Morvidus was still on his horse, six armed thieves appeared from the trees and surrounded him. Even as the best swordsman in the area and on a horse, it was going to be a hopeless fight against six strong, armed, men.

Just as the thieves attacked Morvidus, there was a deafening roar from the forest and a giant bear came thundering towards them. One of the thieves fled instantly back into the trees. The others turned to fight the bear.

Morvidus' horse was terrified. It reared up and threw Morvidus off. One thief attacked Morvidus before he could get up and the two men wrestled on the ground. Elsewhere, there was chaos. The bear had knocked another of the thieves to the ground with one swipe of an enormous paw. It then launched itself onto a second thief, crushing him with the weight of its body. The sound of the thief's bones cracking was enough to send the remaining two thieves running back into the forest, knowing they were beaten.

Meanwhile, Morvidus emerged victorious from his own fight. He pulled himself to his feet and looked at the bear, uncertain if he was to be the next victim. Morvidus stood very still and did not reach for his sword... just yet. The bear approached... and sniffed him... as if it was checking something. Instantly, Morvidus understood. This was his bear, the one whose cub he had released from the trap all those years ago. In fact, Morvidus could see the bear was holding a small piece of the rope he had cut to free the bear cub.

"Thank you, my friend," said Morvidus softly. "We have protected each other." The bear blinked at Morvidus and slowly moved off back into the forest.

Luckily, his horse had not gone far and Morvidus was able to find it quickly. He arrived at the King's fortress in Bagestdon before sunset. The King was impressed when he heard that Morvidus had actually encountered the thieves on the way, and was able to provide important information about them.

Morvidus remembered the King was as fond of hunting large animals as he was of hunting thieves. The last thing Morvidus wanted was for the King to lead a party of warriors to hunt the bear, as well as the thieves. So he kept quiet about the bear. He would only tell Morwenna that bit.

Of course, by leaving out the role of the bear, Morvidus now looked incredibly brave; even braver than he already was. He had apparently singlehandedly fought off six thieves in the forest. To recognise his bravery, the King decided to make Morvidus a knight immediately. "You will need a symbol on your shield now. What will you have, young man?"

"A bear, please, Your Majesty" replied Morvidus promptly.

"And that," finished Dad, "Is the story of how Morvidus put the Bear on his shield, before it eventually became the symbol of Warwickshire."

"Thanks Dad, that was a great story" said Alex, snuggling down for the night. "Do you think turnip ball was how cricket started?"

"Definitely," replied Dad with a wink.

"Morvidus was very brave to free the cub from the trap," continued Alex. "Morvidus and the big bear were both looking after the cub, and then the big bear saved Morvidus later on."

"And don't forget Morvidus protected the grown up bear by not telling the King about him."

"Oh yes," agreed Alex. "He did, didn't he? Everyone looking after each other; like one big Bears' family…."

THE END

EVA T

ROSIE T

ASHTON G

NOAH B

OSCAR M

MADDIE D

ELLIE S

OSCAR W.